The Adventures of Goliath

Goliath at the
Dog Show

The Adventures of Goliath

Goliath at the Dog Show

Terrance Dicks

Illustrated by
Valerie Littlewood

SCHOLASTIC INC.
New York Toronto London Auckland · Sydney

ISBN 0-590-20657-5

Text copyright © 1986 by Terrance Dicks. Illustrations copyright © 1986 by Valerie Littlewood. All rights reserved. Published by Scholastic Inc., 555 Broadway, New York, NY 10012, by arrangement with Barron's Educational Series, Inc.

12 11 10 9 8 7 6 5 4 3 2 1   5 6 7 8 9/9 0/0

Printed in the U.S.A.   40

First Scholastic printing, January 1995

CONTENTS

The Adventures of Goliath

Goliath at the Dog Show

Chapter One

Birth of a Champion

"It was that nice young vet's idea," said the laundromat lady. "When I took Nipper in for his shots, he said Nipper had all the points of a real champion. He said if I entered him in the dog show next week I'd have a real chance of getting Best in Show. There's quite a big cash prize you know, and a cup . . ."

She rattled on, and David listened politely as he stuffed his mother's sheets into the big washing machine.

Nipper was the laundromat lady's dog. As the conversation was going on, he was playing with Goliath, David's dog, outside the shop. This looked rather comical since Nipper, a Jack Russell terrier, was very small while Goliath, a mixture of pretty well everything you could think of, was absolutely enormous.

"When is this dog show?" asked David.

"Next Sunday. They're having it in the Market Hall."

"Well, I wish you and Nipper the best of luck. Maybe I'll enter Goliath as well. I'm sure he'd love a silver cup or a ribbon."

The laundromat lady looked doubtfully at Goliath through the open door. "I'm not sure about that, dear. I mean Goliath is a very nice dog but he is, well . . ." The laundromat lady lowered

3

her voice as if about to say something not quite nice. "He is a mongrel, you know. Nipper's a pedigree dog, you see. And besides, even being purebred isn't enough to make a champion. Everything has to be just right— ears, tail, markings— everything has to look exactly as it should." She paused, trying to be tactful. "You see, dear, Goliath, well he's one of a kind, isn't he? I mean, since he doesn't look like any other kind of dog, there's no way of telling what he's *supposed* to look like, if you see what I mean."

As far as David was concerned, Goliath was supposed to look exactly like Goliath, but he could see there was no use in telling the laundromat lady that.

Promising to come back for the sheets when they were done, David went outside the shop and called Goliath. "Come on you, you silly old thing!"

Putting Goliath on his leash, David walked down to the end of his street and turned right into the main street, busy with Saturday morning shoppers.

"Poor old Goliath," he was thinking. "It isn't fair. Just because he's no particular kind of dog, why shouldn't he have a prize as well?"

By now they were outside the Market Hall, and, sure enough, there was a notice on the board outside announcing the dog show.

David studied it thoughtfully.

As far as he could make out there were individual competitions for all the different breeds and a sort of grand finale contest for the champion of champions: the Best in Show.

"Thinking of entering Goliath?" said a cheery voice behind him.

David turned and saw young Dr. Mackenzie, the new vet.

Dr. Mackenzie was a big, jolly young Australian, quite different from the previous vet, who'd been a rather gloomy sort of character. Now he'd retired and Dr. Mackenzie had taken over.

David said gloomily, "I'd like to enter Goliath if I could. But what for? He hasn't got a pedigree, you know. He's just a mongrel." David's voice was sad. Goliath looked anxiously at him and hung his head, wondering what was wrong.

"Nothing wrong with mongrels, sport," said Dr. Mackenzie heartily. "Tell you the truth, they're my favorite kind of dog. I've got a lot more time for a tough little mongrel than for some of the pampered pedigree dogs I see. You know that Mrs. Gregory?"

David thought. "You mean the one they call the Dog Lady? She's always in the park surrounded by a lot of dogs?"

"That's right. She seems to own about half a dozen, all shapes and sizes, all pedigree and all spoiled rotten. She brought a Peke to see me the other day, said it was ill, not eating much." Dr. Mackenzie laughed. " 'That Peke isn't ill, it's just fat,' I told her. 'Only reason it's not eating is you've stuffed it so full it can't hold any more.' I told her to cut its portions in half, take it down to the

7

park and turn it loose, let it run around with the other dogs, get into a few scraps. 'Course, she was horrified, went off in a huff."

"It's all very well your liking mongrels," said David. "You're not judging the dog show."

"Oh, yes I am," said Dr. Mackenzie. "One of the judges anyway. And I made 'em put in a few special categories this year. Look, there they are down at the bottom here. Best-Trained dog and Best-Groomed dog. Nothing about pedigree there, is there? Why don't you enter Goliath in both of them?"

"I don't know about Best-Trained," said David. "Goliath's got a mind of his own. He knows 'Come' and 'Sit,' and that's about all, and he only does those if he feels like it."

"Well, the dog show's not till a week

from Sunday. That gives you a whole week to get him trained. Besides, there's always Best-Groomed." Dr. Mackenzie bent down and patted Goliath. "Old Goliath here's quite a handsome fella. Give him a bath and a good brushing, and I reckon you'd stand a very good chance!"

Much cheered up, David set off back down the hill to collect his mother's sheets.

He decided to take Dr. Mackenzie's advice and enter Goliath in both classes, Best-Trained and Best-Groomed.

The first was frankly a bit of a gamble. Goliath was probably too scatterbrained to learn much in a week.

Best-Groomed, however, looked much more promising.

Goliath's long white coat could look very handsome if it was properly washed and brushed.

David decided upon his plan.

He would spend as much time as he could spare next week training Goliath.

On the morning of the dog show he would wash Goliath, and brush and comb him until he shone.

Then he'd take him along to the dog show and hope for the best. Maybe Goliath would turn out to be a champion after all. At least they could try.

David spent the next week carrying out his plan.

Every day he took Goliath to the park for a training session.

Every evening he brushed and combed Goliath's long, shaggy coat.

Goliath sat up proudly, rather enjoying all the attention.

He really did look very handsome, thought David.

Maybe Goliath and Nipper would both win prizes, two champions together.

Then Nipper disappeared.

Chapter Two

The Search

David heard the news on the Sunday of the show, just after breakfast. He was out in the park giving Goliath a bit of last-minute training.

So far things hadn't gone too well.

Mind you, it started off all right.

"Sit!" shouted David, and Goliath sat.

"Speak!"

Goliath gave one of his tremendous barks.

"Heel!"

David walked along the path with Goliath trotting sedately by his side.

Goliath quite enjoyed his training sessions, treating them as just another game. He had learned that if he did things right he got lots of fuss, and one of the dog biscuits David carried in his pocket to reward him.

Then came the hardest one. "Sit! Stay!" called David.

Goliath sat, and David walked away without looking back.

Goliath hated this one. He could never understand why David was suddenly abandoning him.

He found it very hard to wait till David stopped, turned, and called, "Come!" and usually rushed off after him long before the word of command.

*   *   *

As David walked away he quite expected to hear the sound of Goliath thundering after him.

But he didn't.

Perhaps Goliath was getting the idea after all, thought David.

Suddenly he heard a chorus of barks, and shouts of "Get away, you great brute!"

David turned and saw that Goliath

had rushed off, not after him but in the other direction, toward the Dog Lady, who had appeared in the park surrounded by her usual gang of pedigree dogs.

There was a Pekinese, a Jack Russell, or was it two Jack Russells, a pair of Scotties, and two Skye terriers.

They were all on long leashes—the Dog Lady never let her dogs off—and at the moment they were all whirling in a mad merry-go-round with Goliath and the Dog Lady somewhere in the middle.

David dashed up, grabbed Goliath by the collar, and heaved him away. "I'm terribly sorry," he gasped.

"I should think so, too," shouted the Dog Lady, a tall imposing figure wrapped in an expensive fur coat. "These are all valuable pedigree dogs, young man. Several of them are appearing in

the dog show this afternoon. I cannot have their nerves shattered by the attacks of that horrible great hairy mongrel of yours. If you can't keep it under control I shall complain to the police."

Disentangling her dog leashes, she stalked away angrily.

David looked reprovingly at Goliath. "Bad dog, Goliath. You know she hates you going near her wretched dogs. What's got into you?"

This wasn't their first brush with the Dog Lady, who was always complaining about the way other dogs behaved.

Goliath was quite terrified of her—he hated being shouted at—and usually he kept well away.

David was just about to start Goliath's obedience training again when he saw the lady from the laundromat hurrying

toward them. To his astonishment she was alone.

"Hullo," said David. "Where's Nipper?"

"I only wish I knew! He ran off early this morning, and I can't find him anywhere. You haven't seen him, have you?"

David shook his head. "I'll keep an eye out for you. Nipper will probably come running up if he spots Goliath."

Nipper was an active little dog, and the laundromat lady couldn't always give him all the exercise he needed.

Recently Nipper had taken to wandering off, roaming through the park on his own, and then trotting back home when he was tired. Since he always did come back, the laundromat lady had stopped worrying about it.

The laundromat lady gave David a worried look.

"You don't think Nipper's been . . ."

"Dognapped again?" David shook his head. "The ones who did it before wouldn't dare try it again. They'd be the first ones the police would be after, wouldn't they?"

"Besides," David said, "you haven't had any ransom notes or phone calls have you?"

"No, there's been nothing like that."

"I'm sure he's just wandered off," said David consolingly. "I only hope he turns up in time for the show."

The laundromat lady went off to look for Nipper.

David promised that he'd look, too, and get in touch with her as soon as he heard any news.

Taking the opposite direction from the laundromat lady, David and Goliath searched all that part of the park.

Nipper was nowhere to be found.

Chapter Three

The Show

Finally, David decided he'd have to give up the search.

He felt very sorry for the laundromat lady, but he couldn't really believe Nipper had been stolen again. That would be like lightning striking in the same place twice.

And if Nipper hadn't been stolen, then he was just lost and would no doubt turn up sooner or later.

It was Goliath that David had to

worry about now. He had been really hurt by the suggestion that Goliath was somehow worthless because he was only a mongrel. If there was any way hard work could earn Goliath a prize, David was determined to do his very best.

It was lunchtime by the time David got home, and right after lunch he started preparing Goliath for his day of glory.

By special permission he was allowed to bathe Goliath in the real bathtub.

He lathered him thoroughly with special dog shampoo, rinsed him clean with the shower attachment, getting all the shampoo off, then rubbed him dry with an old towel, finishing him off with his mother's hairdryer.

Then he brushed and combed Goliath until his arms ached and Goliath's white coat was spotless and silky.

When David had finished, his mother and father looked on in admiration. "I think Goliath looks really beautiful," said David's mother. "I hope you win."

"You certainly deserve to after all that hard work," said David's father. "Come on, I'll drive you up to the hall. Can't risk a speck of dust getting on Goliath on the way!"

They stopped at the laundromat to ask if there was any news of Nipper and found the lady nearly in tears. "He's still missing. I've been all over the park and to the police and everything."

"Never mind," said David's mother consolingly. "I'm sure he'll turn up. Why don't you come to the dog show with us anyway? You can leave a note on the door saying where you are, and then if someone brings him back you'll be in the right place."

"That's right," said David's father. "Better than sitting here by yourself worrying. Who knows, maybe David and Goliath will be able to pull off another miracle and find Nipper for you!"

Finally, they persuaded her to come. She got in the back of the car with David and the shining white Goliath, and they went off to the Market Hall.

It was a huge building, rather like an airplane hangar. On weekdays and Saturdays there was a whole market inside with rows and rows of stalls selling everything you could think of, but today the stalls had all been cleared away.

The room had been divided into rings, with tables for the judges, and all around the walls there were dogs and dog owners waiting for their turn.

There was a refreshment stall, too, and

other stalls selling various doggy articles.
There was a curtained-off area for the
judges and committee members. David
caught sight of Dr. Mackenzie appearing
from behind the curtain and joining his
fellow judges at a table.

He caught David's eye, looked
admiringly at Goliath, and gave David a
broad grin and a thumbs-up sign.

David's father bought three cups of
tea, a soda, and a program, and they
waited while the various breeds and
classes were judged. There were large

dogs, small dogs, everything from
Mastiffs and St. Bernards to Pekinese
and Chihuahuas, all looking beautifully
groomed and very aristocratic.

David's heart sank. What on earth
were he and Goliath doing among such
a distinguished crowd?

The last three events on the
program were the competitions for
Best-Trained, Best-Groomed, and finally
Best in Show.

Goliath was entered for the first two,
and Nipper of course would have been in
the third, if only he'd been there.

"All contestants to the main ring for
Best-Trained Dog," called the
loudspeaker voice.

The rules of this particular
competition were that each contestant
was to demonstrate the dog's obedience
training as he or she chose, rather than

going through a set course.

David's turn came last, and nervously he led Goliath into the ring.

To his surprise there was an approving murmur from the judges and the crowd.

Goliath certainly looked very impressive in his highly groomed state. Perhaps they all thought he was some rare breed of giant dog, not a mongrel at all.

David began to work through the commands he and Goliath had practiced.

"Sit!"

Goliath sat.

"Heel!"

Goliath walked around the ring to heel.

"Speak!"

Goliath gave a bark that shook the hall.

"Beg!"

Goliath sat up and begged, and there was a round of applause.

David drew a deep breath and began the last and most difficult command. "Sit!" Goliath sat. "Stay!"

David turned and walked away, hoping desperately that Goliath wouldn't follow him and ruin everything.

He had almost reached the far side of

the ring when there came a pattering of feet going *away* from him and a chorus of frantic barking.

David turned around and gasped in horror at what he saw.

It was the morning all over again.

There was the Dog Lady, surrounded by her crowd of leashed dogs, all tangled up with Goliath in the middle.

"This is disgraceful," she was shrieking. "I was just on my way to prepare for Best in Show when this brute attacked us. My dogs' nerves will be ruined!"

Feeling trapped in a repeating nightmare, David went and tugged Goliath away, and the Dog Lady was led away too, still protesting.

David stood looking on miserably as a sheepdog was awarded Best-Trained Dog.

"Cheer up, youngster," said a familiar voice. It was Dr. Mackenzie.

"To be honest, that sheepdog was in the lead anyway. And there's still Best-Groomed. You've got a good chance there I reckon."

In the distance they could hear the high-pitched voice of the Dog Lady still protesting.

"That wretched woman and her dogs," said David. "The trouble is it's the second time today that's happened. I don't know what's got into Goliath!"

"Ah, don't worry about her," said Dr. Mackenzie. "The old duck's a bit strung up, see, this is a big day for her. That Skye terrier of hers has won Best in Show two years running. If he does it a third time, she gets to keep the cup." He patted David on the back. "Cheer up, Goliath may win a prize yet."

For a time it seemed as if Dr. Mackenzie was right.

There was a ripple of amusement as Goliath walked around the ring, parading before the judges with the other contestants.

It looked as if his bad behavior wasn't being held against him anyway.

David's hopes were quite high as they passed the judges' table. Then he saw one of the judges, a fierce-looking lady in a tweed hat, lean forward, peer at Goliath, and point something out to her fellow judges. David saw them nod in agreement, even Dr. Mackenzie.

A few minutes later David stood looking on disappointedly as the Best-Groomed Dog award went to a smug-looking Sealyham.

"What went wrong?" he asked Dr. Mackenzie as he came back from the judges' table.

Dr. Mackenzie sighed. "Bad luck, kid. I wanted you to win, but the standard of grooming is very high, and once they spotted that smudge on Goliath's coat . . ."

"What smudge?" demanded David. "That coat was spotless."

Dr. Mackenzie bent down and lifted Goliath's chin. "This one, right here on his chest."

Goliath looked shamefaced.

David knelt down to look, and sure enough, there was a smear of black, right across the snowy white fur of Goliath's chest. David stared at it in astonishment. "Where did that come from? It's impossible . . ."

He heard the voice of the Dog Lady from across the hall, where she was standing with her Skye terrier, waiting

to enter it for Best in Show, waiting for the prize she was certain of winning for the third time in succession.

Suddenly everything fell into place.

David knew what had happened to Nipper.

He knew exactly where Nipper was now.

And he knew just what he was going to do about it.

Chapter Four

The Winner

Dr. Mackenzie was already turning away, and David grabbed his sleeve.

"Listen, have you got a minute?"

"Not really. I've got to get ready to help judge the Best in Show."

"This is something to do with Best in Show, something you really ought to know about."

Dr. Mackenzie gave him a puzzled look. "Okay then, but make it snappy will you?"

As quickly as he could, David told him the story of Nipper's disappearance and his own theory about what had happened.

Dr. Mackenzie listened in amazement. "The old witch! I bet she would, too. This has got to be looked into. I'm going to tell the committee right away."

"No, wait," said David. "I've got a better idea."

He told Dr. Mackenzie his plan.

Dr. Mackenzie chuckled. "It's a great idea, if we can pull it off."

He paused. "But just suppose you're wrong? You could end up in real trouble!"

"I'll risk it," said David confidently. "Anyway, I'm not wrong."

"Good for you, sport," said Dr. Mackenzie. "Right, then, I'll distract her while you do the dirty deed. Then I'll meet you in the judges' area, behind that curtain. There's everything we need there, and some of the other owners will help as well. It's about time that old witch got what was coming to her."

He strode away. David saw him go up to the Dog Lady and engage her in conversation.

The Dog Lady began shaking her head indignantly and started fishing in her handbag for some papers.

Very soon she and Dr. Mackenzie

were engaged in a heated argument, and David felt it was time to act.

Handing Goliath over to his puzzled parents he began sidling closer to the Dog Lady.

By now she had just one dog on the leash, the famous Skye terrier that had already won Best in Show twice.

Her other dogs were tethered to a hook at the side of the Market Hall, on the wall just behind her.

It was the same group of dogs David and Goliath had met in the park— the remaining Skye terrier, the Peke, the two Scotties, and the two Jack Russells. David studied these last two with keen interest. One was a bright, perky-looking animal, not unlike Nipper, though without the distinctive markings.

The other Jack Russell didn't resemble Nipper at all. It was a bedraggled, cross-looking animal with a good deal more black in its coat than was usual. Instead of Nipper's black eye patch, most of this dog's face was black, and the saddle marking on its back was so large that it covered most of the little dog's body. All the same, this was the dog that David was interested in. He crept quietly up to it and unhooked its leash from its collar. The little dog wagged its tail furiously as he picked it up, licking his face and whining a welcome.

"Sssh!" whispered David.

Bundling the little dog under his coat, he hurried away.

As he moved off he could hear the Dog Lady saying, "So you see, Dr. Mackenzie, my entry forms were in in plenty of time. You don't think I'd get something like that wrong, surely? Not when my little

Skye Prince is going to win Best in Show for the third time in succession!"

"I'm so sorry," said Dr. Mackenzie humbly. "I must have mixed up the dates. Do excuse me, I must go and get ready for the judging."

Dr. Mackenzie hurried over to the curtained-off judges' area where David was waiting for him.

He took the little dog from David's arms. "This is the little fella, is it? Don't worry, we'll soon have him fixed up. You go and get your friend ready and standing by, and I'll get things moving here." David ducked back outside the curtain and headed for the refreshment tent where the laundromat lady and his parents were drinking still more cups of tea.

David hurried over to the laundromat lady and said, "You'd better finish your tea and get ready."

She stared at him. "Ready for what?"

"For the Best in Show contest of course."

"But Nipper isn't here!"

"Oh, yes, he is," said David. "At least, he is and he isn't. But he'll be here soon."

Suddenly, he wondered if there would be enough time to carry out the last stages of his plan.

As if in answer to his thought the loudspeaker crackled into life. "There will be a short delay before the Best in Show contest. One of the competitors has been delayed, and owing to quite exceptional circumstances the judges have decided to allow him a little more time."

David relaxed. "That's all right then, you've got time to finish your tea. Any chance of a soda and something to eat?"

David's father bought him a soda and a bag of potato chips. "I must say you seem remarkably cheerful, especially since poor old Goliath lost both his events."

"Oh, well, can't win 'em all," said David cheerfully. "Someone else is about to find that out as well."

"What on earth are you talking about?" asked his mother.

David tossed Goliath a chip. "Just you wait and see, mom. It shouldn't be very long now."

About ten minutes later the loudspeaker said, "All contestants for Best in Show to the main ring, please. The judging is about to begin."

Already the judges were taking their places at the table.

David grabbed the laundromat lady's arm and led her over to the curtain. Just as they reached it a young lady appeared from behind it—with Nipper on a leash.

She handed the leash to David. "Here you are—he's been washed, dried, and groomed in record time. Good luck!"

David looked down at Nipper, who was so clean and so well-groomed that he positively shone. He handed the astonished laundromat lady the leash.

She took it and knelt down beside

Nipper, fussing over him delightedly.

"What happened? Where did you find him?"

"No time to explain," said David. "Time you were in that ring— come on!"

He bustled her over to where the contestants were assembling.

At the sight of Nipper, the Dog Lady's mouth opened wide. She turned to look for the rest of her dogs, but before she could say anything the contest was beginning.

David and his parents watched delightedly as Nipper was paraded around the ring with all the other dogs.

There was a murmur of approval from the crowd, and the judges looked just as impressed.

Before very long it was over, and Nipper had won Best in Show.

The Dog Lady was furious—and she

seemed frightened as well.

Without a word to anyone she snatched up the leashes of her little group of dogs and almost dragged them out of the Market Hall.

"What was all that about?" asked David's father.

"I imagine she's ashamed of herself," said David.

"Why, just because she lost?"

"No, because she stole Nipper so as to be sure of winning."

"*She* stole Nipper?" asked David's mother in amazement.

David nodded. "Borrowed would be more like it, I suppose. She must have gathered from Dr. Mackenzie that Nipper was a serious rival. She was desperate to win a third time and keep the cup. Desperate enough to dognap Nipper just to keep him from entering the show. I expect she'd have given him back once the show was over."

"Where did she put him?" asked David's father.

"That was the clever bit. She didn't dare leave him alone in case someone found him, and she didn't dare ask anyone to look after him. So she hid Nipper here, under all our noses. She just disguised him with some black dye and hid him in the middle of her own dogs. That's why Goliath kept making a dash for them—he knew Nipper was in among them, and he was trying to tell me."

David patted Goliath's head. "Luckily some of the dye rubbed off on him during that last fuss. It lost us Best-Groomed Dog, but it made me realize what had happened to Nipper."

Dr. Mackenzie bustled over to them.

"Just come over to the main ring will you, David—and bring Goliath."

David went over to the ring where Nipper was proudly sporting his winner's ribbon.

The laundromat lady promptly hugged and kissed him, much to his embarrassment. She was almost weeping with pride and pleasure.

Dr. Mackenzie raised his voice. "Ladies and gentlemen! Owing to some most unusual circumstances, the judges have decided to make a Special Award this year. The award is for the most unforgettable and the most characterful dog, and the winner is— Goliath!"

There was a tremendous cheer from the crowd, and everyone clapped as David led Goliath up to the judges' table to collect his award—the biggest ribbon the judges had been able to lay their hands on.

David tied the ribbon to Goliath's collar, and there was another cheer.

As Nipper and Goliath posed proudly for the local newspaper's photographer, David thought that Goliath had got his award just for being Goliath—which was just as it should be!

Other ADVENTURES OF GOLIATH
that you will enjoy reading:

About the author

After studying at Cambridge, Terrance Dicks became
an advertising copy-writer, then a radio and television
scriptwriter and script editor. His career as a
children's author began with the *Dr Who* series and he
has now written a variety of other books on subjects
ranging from horror to detection.